This book belongs to

____

Ceterra Mance is a wife, mother, aunt, sister, friend, and teacher. She has her master's degree in curriculum and instruction, and has taught elementary school for 10 years.

She also crochets, makes herbal tea, writes poems, sews, draws terribly, does puzzles, braids hair, and any other random hobby that strikes her.

She wrote this book for Jayveon, Taliyah (Tilly Rose), T'Kyron, Cheranii, Cornelius Jr., Iyana, Daniel, Brooklyn, Benjamin, and every child she's ever taught; just to show them they could accomplish whatever they wanted in life.

ISBN: ISBN: 979-8-218-24539-9
Written by Ceterra Mance

Illustrated by Taranggana

Knot Fhairies

Written by
Ceterra Mance

Illustrated by
Taranggana

DREAM
Tilly Rose woke up excited to go to school today.

Her mother had spent a good amount of time combing and twisting her curly hair. It took a few hours from wash to finish, but now she was ready to show up and show out.

She went to brush her teeth and wash her face for the day, but when she looked in the mirror, her bonnet was missing, and her hair
was a mess.

"Mommy!" she screamed in a panic.
How could this have happened?

When she went to bed last night,
everything looked perfectly normal!

"What's wrong, Tilly?" her mother asked, quickly entering the restroom.

Tears welled up in Tilly's eyes. "Why does my **HAIR** look like this? It took so much effort to make it just right. I put on my bonnet just like you showed me."

"Well, little Rose, it seems the No Good KNOT FHAIRIES had a great time last night. They got you!"

"If they're not **FAIRIES**, then what are they? Whoever they are, they're definitely no good," Tilly said, wiping her eyes and sighing sadly. She knew Mommy could help her sort out the mess on top of her head.

"Let me explain who the **KNOT FHAIRIES** are," Mommy said, leading Tilly Rose to her room.

The KNOT FHAIRIES live in the vents in the ceiling, the cracks in the corners, or the windows that need sealing.

Once they find a tiny home
that has what they enjoy,
it's hard to get rid of
them – they always play coy.

These shy little friends wait for the evening to come to sneak around and play, but they do no thieving.

They love to frolic,
and they love to play,
in the coils and curls of
children as they lay

Asleep in their beds, and while you dream,

they swim in your tresses like a lake or a stream.

They build castles and play hide and seek

in freshly oiled scalps, they sled and they shriek.

Sometimes, however, and this is important
they leave behind a mess for you, that's unfortunate.

They will leave behind traces, though they never get caught.
you can see the evidence in your FAIRY KNOTS.

The only way to protect your so fresh and so clean style is to wear a **BONNET** or **SCARF**, because all the while...

DREAM

They will slip and slide on silk and satin. If you wrap your hair up, the **FHAIRIES** can't get in.

If you do it just so, it won't fall off at night, and when you wake up, your hair will be just right.

So, you can start your day with your crown
on straight, and your glorious smile beaming,
with an attitude that's great.

As Mommy completed the finishing touches to Tilly Rose's style, she said, "See, you look as good as new. Hold your head up no matter what and know that you are loved! Even by the KNOT FHAIRIES!"
BLUE MAGIC

Tilly thanked her mommy and finished getting dressed for school. She couldn't wait to show her friends her pretty hair and her positive attitude.
Although, she knew she would have to warn several of her classmates about the KNOT FHAIRIES.

"Tonight," Tilly thought with a smile on her face, "I will ask for help to make sure I am wearing my bonnet correctly. I have to protect my hair from the **KNOT FHAIRIES!**"